Humpty Dumpty

Written by Catherine Baker
Illustrated by Helen Flook

Collins

2

3

4

6

8

10

12

What happened to Humpty Dumpty?

After reading

Letters and Sounds: Phase 1

Word count: 0

Curriculum links: EYFS: Self-confidence and self-awareness: children are confident to try new activities

Early learning goals: Listening and attention: children listen attentively in a range of situations; Understanding: children answer 'how' and 'why' questions about their experiences and in response to stories or events

Developing fluency

- Encourage your child to hold the book and turn the pages.
- Ensure that your child understands that the book is about the Humpty Dumpty rhyme and that they can recognise the elements from the rhyme on each page.
- Can they also spot characters and things from other nursery rhymes? (e.g. *Mary Mary Quite Contrary, Bo Peep, Three Blind Mice*)
- Look at the pictures together and encourage your child to talk about what is happening in each picture, giving as much detail as they can.

Phonic practice

- Together, look for objects in the pictures that make sounds. (e.g. *a horse clip clopping, a bird singing*) Ask your child to try and copy these sounds using voice sounds, percussion and body percussion.
- Look for rhyming words in the pictures. (e.g. *sheep, Bo Peep, steep; hat, cat, bat*) Ask your child if they can think of any other rhyming words.
- Look for opportunities to explore alliteration, by focusing on things in the pictures that begin with 'sh' on pages 2–3, 'p' on pages 4–5, 'b' on pages 6–7, 'c' on pages 8–9, 'p' on pages 10–11, and 's' on pages 12–13.

Extending vocabulary

- Talk about the pictures in circles at the bottom of the pages. Ask your child to tell you what they see. Can they spot the objects in the main picture?
- Discuss words for all of the things children can see in the pictures. Ask them to point out anything they don't recognise. Tell them the word for it and explain what it is.